AGAIN

Emily Gravett

MACMILLAN CHILDREN'S BOOKS

For Kian, Louis, Wayne and Terry

First published in 2011 by Macmillan Children's Books
a division of Macmillan Publishers Limited
20 New Wharf Road, London NI 9RR
Basingstoke and Oxford
www.panmacmillan.com
Associated companies worldwide
ISBN 978-0-230-74536-0
Text and Illustrations copyright © Emily Gravett, 2011
The right of Emily Gravett to be identified as the Author and Illustrator
of this work has been asserted in accordance
with the Copyright, Designs and Patents Act 1988
All rights reserved.
No part of this publication may be reproduced
or transmitted in any form, or by any means without permission.

1 3 5 7 9 8 6 4 2

A CIP catalogue record for this book is available from the British Library
Printed in China

For Kian, Louis, Wayne and Terry

First published in 2011 by Macmillan Children's Books
a division of Macmillan Publishers Limited
20 New Wharf Road, London N1 9RR
Basingstoke and Oxford
www.panmacmillan.com
Associated companies worldwide
ISBN 978-0-230-74536-0
Text and Illustrations copyright © Emily Gravett, 2011
The right of Emily Gravett to be identified as the Author and Illustrator
of this work has been asserted in accordance
with the Copyright, Designs and Patents Act 1988

1 3 5 7 9 8 6 4 2

A CIP catalogue record for this book is available from the British Library
Printed in China

AGAIN!

Emily Gravett

MACMILLAN CHILDREN'S BOOKS

It was nearly bedtime.

Cedric the dragon's a bright angry red.
He's never,
His whole life,
(Not once) been to bed.

At night-time when everyone else is asleep,
He noisily prowls through the tower, then leaps
Down to the bridge to be nasty and sly,
And torment the trolls (who by nature are shy).

When that makes him hungry he takes to the skies,
Grabbing princesses to turn into pies,
Or occasionally crumbles, or sometimes just toast
(If crumbles or pies would take too long to roast).

At the end of each day he shouts out this refrain:
"TOMORROW I'LL DO IT ALL OVER AGAIN!"

Again?

Cedric the dragon's a bright angry red.
He's never,
His whole life,
(Not once) been to bed.

At night-time when Cedric SHOULD be asleep,
He noisily stomps through the tower, then leaps
Down to the bridge to say a big sorry
For teasing the trolls (who do tend to worry).

When that makes him hungry he takes out a pie
Which he shares with the trolls. Then, heaving a sigh,
He goes home to his tower
And shouts out this refrain:
"TOMORROW I'LL DO IT ALL OVER AGAIN!"

AGAIN!

Cedric the dragon's a big sleepyhead.
He's decided it's time
HE WAS REALLY IN BED.

He's made friends with the princess
And wished her goodnight,
The trolls are all happy,
The moon is out bright.

Now I'm closing the book and saying quite plain:

"TOMORROW I'll read it all over again."

AGAIN!

AGAIN!

Cedric the dragon *is no longer red,*
As Cedric . . .
the dragon's . . . asleep
. . . in . . . his . . . be . . . z z z   z

Z Z Z z z z z z z z z z z z z z z z z z z

AGAIN!
AGAIN!
AGAIN!

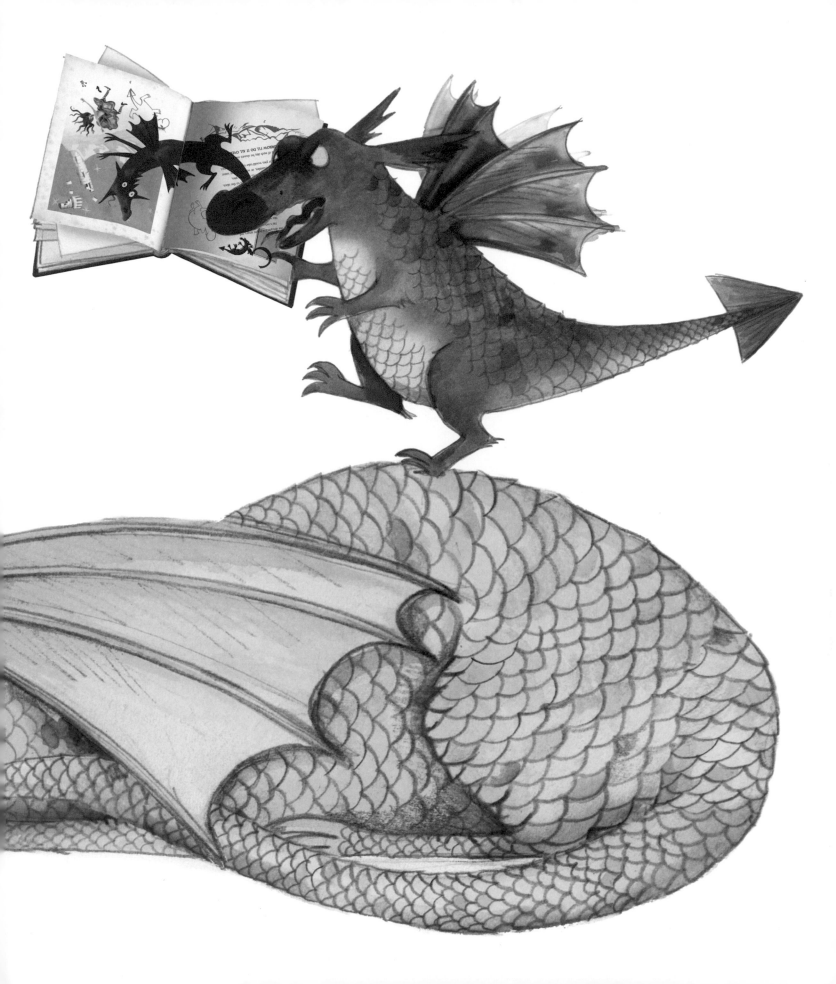

AGAIN! AGAIN

AGAIN AGAIN

AGAIN AGAIN

AGAIN!

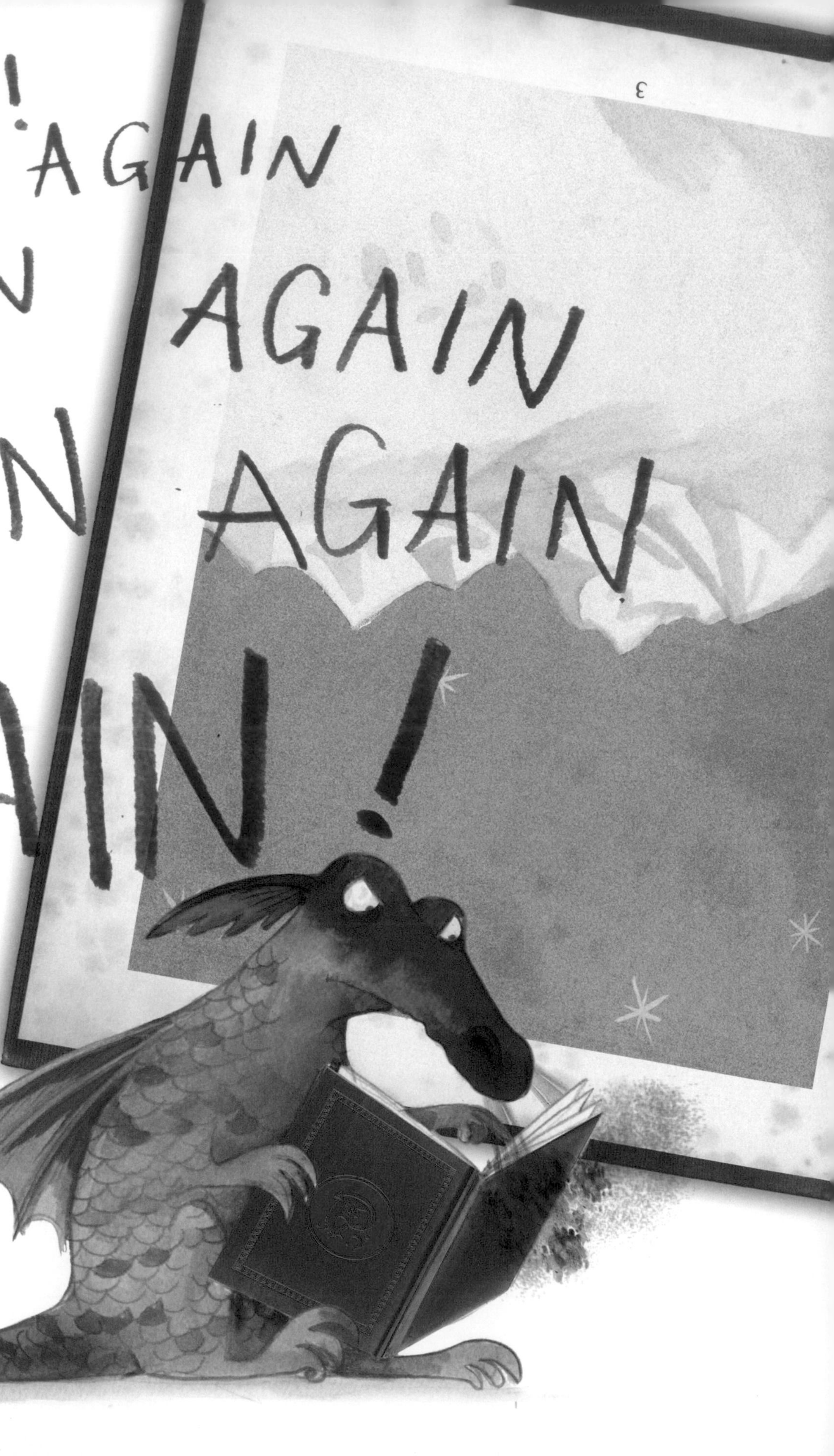